Song of the Stars
A Christmas Story

By Sally Lloyd-Jones

Paintings by Alison Jay

ZONDERVAN.com/
AUTHORTRACKER
follow your favorite authors

For Mark and Yolie with love
—SL-J

For Anne. Happy Christmas
Love from Alison

ZONDERKIDZ

Song of the Stars
Copyright © 2011 by Sally Lloyd-Jones
Paintings © 2011 by Alison Jay

Requests for information should be addressed to:
Zonderkidz, *Grand Rapids, Michigan 49530*

ISBN 978-0-310-72291-5

Editor: Barbara Herndon
Art direction: Jody Langley

Printed in China

11 12 13 14 15 16 /LPC/ 6 5 4 3 2 1

Song of the Stars

The world was about to change forever.
And it almost went by unnoticed ...

But the leaves, that night,
rustled with a rumor.
News rang out across the open fields.
A song drifted over the hills.

The wind whispered it softly
in the sycamore trees
that waved their moonlit branches
to the sky.

A barn owl took flight.

Woodland creatures stirred ...

"It's time! It's time!"

In the pinewoods, two deer raised their heads.

A big brown bear sniffed the air.

A red fox darted.

The faces of little flowers lifted
to the skies …

"It's time! It's time!"

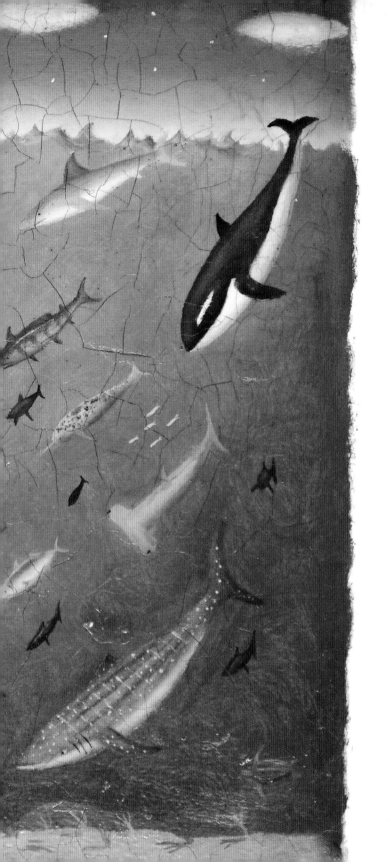

The skies shouted it to the
seas that thundered it to
the waves that roared it to
the great white whales
that sang it to the starfish
in the deep.

And tiny sandpipers danced it
on shining sands ...

"It's time! It's time!"

The running rivers bounded over boulders
and the otters clapped and played and sang to
the ducklings that splashed and quacked to
the salmon that leaped and leaped.

And tiny field mice
and insects and little creeping things
and sparrows and robins

and every single blade of grass
squeaked and hummed and
chirped and sang ...

"It's time! It's time!"

Wild stallions drummed it to the ground ...

"Get ready! Get ready! Be glad! Be glad!"

On a lonely peak
a lion raised his strong head
and roared it out
to the empty wilderness ...

"The Mighty King!
The Prince of Peace!"

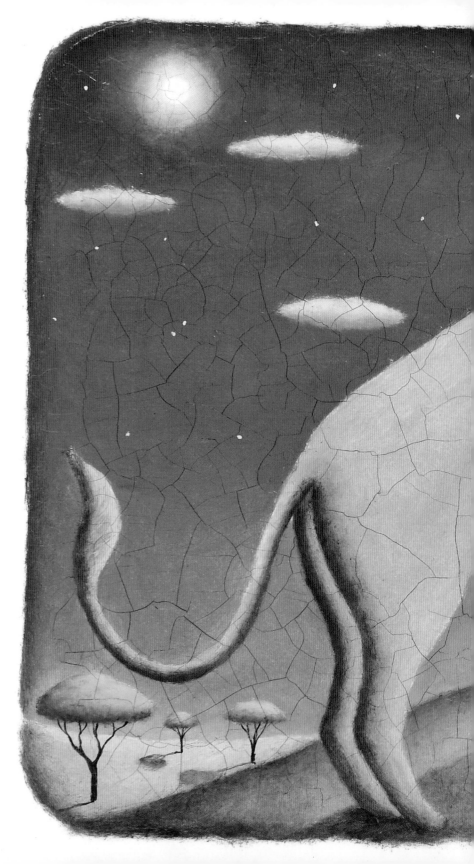

All the stars joined together
in a chorus that rang out through the heavens …

"The Bright and Morning Star!"

And on a hillside overlooking a little town
sheep nuzzled their new lambs ...

"The Good Shepherd!"

Suddenly angels lit up the whole sky
and a great choir sang it out loud …

"It's time! He's come!
At last! He's here!"

And in the little town
in a little shed
in a little window
a candle flickered in the dark.

And a tiny cry rang out
in the cold night air.

And high above
a single star
set in the highest heavens
shone out brighter than all the others
and poured down silver
onto the little shed ...

"A Light to light up
the whole world!"

The animals stood around his bed.
And the whole earth
and all the stars and sky
held its breath ...

"The One who made us
has come to live with us!"

And a young mother
with no place to rest
nowhere to stay
kept it as a song
inside her heart ...

"Our Rescuer!"

And they gazed in wonder
at God's great gift.

Lying on a bed of straw
wrapped in rags—

a tiny little baby.

Heaven's Son
sleeping under the stars
that he made.